"Jack Fritscher writes wond

"Jack Fritscher has roamed the furthest corners of sexuality, and can lead you on head trips unequaled by any other gay writer I know of. You may resist, as I did, some of the aggression, machismo, and sexual practices only to be won over by Fritscher's prose....[He] writes with sweat and wit, dirt and desire. Fritscher is a knee to the groin."
—John F. Karr, *Bay Area Reporter*, San Francisco

"Fritscher reads brilliantly." —*San Francisco Chronicle*

Fritscher "is proof that gay erotic writing can also be rousing good literature, stimulating the mental as much as it does the physical. Author Fritscher, who wrote the first and best book on Robert Mapplethorpe several years ago, laces his rough-and-tumble erotics with supple brawny prose; he's a master wordsmith, crafting his tales of muscle and passion... with an imagination rare for the milieu."
—Richard Labonté, A Different Light

"Fritscher is the master of gay fiction."
—Larry Townsend, author, *The Leatherman's Handbook*

"The wit of Fritscher's characters' banter is matched by the text, offering much in the way of intelligent observation and wry commentary on the social milieu of the first-class passengers and crew and the disaster itself....Fritscher shows a greater degree of sensitivity to history and the story of *Titanic* than many other writers who have used *Titanic* to make socio-political points, or as dramatic backdrop for turgid carrying on." —www.bytenet.net/TitanicImprint.com

"All the News That's Fit to Print"

The New York Times.

TITANIC SINKS FOUR HOURS AFTER HITTING ICEBERG;
866 RESCUED BY CARPATHIA, PROBABLY 1250 PERISH;
ISMAY SAFE, MRS. ASTOR MAYBE, NOTED NAMES MISSING

The Lost Titanic Being Towed Out of Belfast Harbor.

PARTIAL LIST OF THE SAVED.

CAPT. E. J. SMITH.

TITANIC
The Untold Tale of Gay Passengers and Crew

100th Anniversary Collectors' Edition

Jack Fritscher

Palm Drive Publishing

For author history and literary research:
www. JackFritscher.com

Published by Palm Drive Publishing, San Francisco CA
EMail: correspond@PalmDrivePublishing.com

Fritscher, Jack 1939-
    Titanic! The Untold Tale of the Gay Passengers and Crew/ Jack Fritscher
    p. cm.
    ISBN-13 978-1-890834-08-1
    ISBN-eBook 978-1-890834-60-9
    1. American Literature—20th Century. 2. Homosexuality—Fiction.
    3. Gay Studies—Fiction. 4. Erotica—Gay. 5. Sadomasochism—Fiction.
    6. Titanic—Fiction.

Printed in the United States of America
First Printing, January 2012
10 9 8 7 6 5 4 3 2 1

Palm Drive Publishing®
San Francisco CA
www.PalmDrivePublishing.com

Epigraph

Walt Whitman, As If *Titanic*

Now, Voyager, sail thou forth, to seek and find...

What think you I take my pen in hand to record?
The...ship, perfect-model'd, majestic, that I saw pass the
offing to-day under full sail?
...of two simple men I saw to-day on the pier in the midst
of the crowd, parting the parting of dear friends,
The one to remain hung on the other's neck and
passionately kiss'd him,
While the one to depart tightly prest the one to remain in his arms.

I am for those who believe in loose delights.
I share the midnight orgies of young men.
I dance with the dancers and drink with the drinkers.

I ascend to the foretruck,
I take my place late at night in the crow's-nest,
We sail the arctic sea, it is plenty light enough,
Through the clear atmosphere I stretch around
on the wonderful beauty,
The enormous masses of ice pass me and I pass them,
the scenery is plain in all directions,
The white-topt mountains show in the distance,
I fling out my fancies toward them,
We are approaching some great battle-field
in which we are soon to be engaged...
Sea of the brine of life and of unshovell'd yet always-ready graves...

The conductor beats time for the band,
and all the performers follow him.

I understand the large hearts of heroes,
The courage of present times and all times,
How the skipper saw the crowded and rudderless wreck of the
steamship, and Death chasing it up and down...
How he knuckled tight...
How he saved the drifting company at last,
How the lank loose-gown'd women look'd when boated from the
side of their prepared graves,
How the silent old-faced infants and the lifted sick, and the
sharp-lipp'd unshaved men;
All this I swallow...it becomes mine,
I am the man, I suffer'd, I was there.

Near by, the corpse of the child that serv'd in the cabin;
The dead face of an old salt with long white hair and
carefully curl'd whiskers.
Blind loving wrestling touch, sheath'd hooded sharp-tooth'd touch!
Did it make you ache so, leaving me?

They fetch my man's body up dripping and drown'd.

Now, land and life, finale and farewell,
Now, Voyager, depart...
Often enough hast thou adventur'd o'er the seas,
Cautiously cruising... But now...Embrace thy friends...
To port...no more returning,
Depart upon thy endless cruise, old Sailor.

Out of the rolling ocean, the crowd, came a drop gently to me,
Whispering "I love you," before long I die,
I have travel'd a long way merely to look on you to touch you,
For I could not die till I once look'd on you,
For I fear'd I might afterward lose you.
Now we have met, we have look'd, we are safe,
Return in peace to the ocean, my love,
I too am part of that ocean, my love,...
as for me, for you, the irresistible sea is to separate us,
As for an hour carrying us diverse, yet cannot carry us diverse forever;

Be not impatient—a little space—know you I salute the air,
the ocean and the land,
Every day at sundown for your dear sake, my love.

Vivas...to those whose...vessels sank in the sea!
And to those themselves who sank in the sea!

You sea! I resign myself to you also—I guess what you mean;
I behold from the beach your crooked inviting fingers;
I believe you refuse to go back without feeling of me;
We must have a turn together—I undress—hurry me
out of sight of the land;
Cushion me soft, rock me in billowy drowse;
Dash me with amorous wet—I can repay you.

Now, voyager!

—Walt Whitman, *Leaves of Grass*

Walt Whitman (1819-1892), the great gay poet, broke the boundaries of poetic form, and rearranged and added to his ever growing book *Leaves of Grass* with every edition from his first in 1855 to his death-bed edition of 1891. Always writing about the human condition, Whitman often invoked the universal sea, ship wrecks, heroism, homosexual love, and loss. In his excerpting his beloved Whitman, Fritscher, without altering the beat of Whitman's "Drum Taps," samples *Leaves of Grass* as if Whitman, the American pop-culture poet, were alive to chronicle, as he surely would have done, the sinking of *Titanic* which occurred twenty years after Whitman's death. All the words sampled are Whitman's alone.

WHITE STAR LINE

BOARDING PASS

PERMISSION GRANTED TO COME ABOARD

WHITE STAR LINE'S

R.M.S.

TITANIC

ISMAY, IMRIE & CO.,
34, LEADENHALL STREET, LONDON,

10, WATER STREET, LIVERPOOL.

Foreword

Titanic:
How the Boys in the Band Played On
Reclaiming the Gay History of *Titanic*

On a night so clear that passengers could see stars reflecting on a sea smooth as a mirror, *Titanic*, the grandest ship in the whole wide world, broke in two, reared up high as a skyscraper, lights burning brilliantly, and sank into the depths of archetypal myth. That night on that sea, 2200 people, including 400 gay passengers and crew, watched *Titanic* go down. Only 700 of those thousands were in lifeboats. Fifteen hundred died around them. The story telling began...

* * * *

Breaking the straight trance of received *Titanic* history, San Francisco author Jack Fritscher reclaims gay history by writing a pitch-perfect sex epic of gay survival. *Titanic* "outs" the forbidden gay love story of the world's most famous cruise, featuring the Unsinkable Molly Brown, the posh lovers Michael Whitney and Edward Wedding, and the working crew including the rugged Balkan Stoker, the redheaded Royal Purser Felix Jones, and the ship's second carpenter Michael Brice and Third Officer Sam Maxwell.

Titanic sank April 15, 1912, creating a media frenzy. Fritscher said, "In movie-newsreel footage shot three days later on the deck of the rescue ship *Carpathia* immediately after it docked at Chelsea Piers in New York, a dozen of the surviving *Titanic* crew, mostly sailor lads in tight white pants hiding little, showing lots, can be seen in very intimate horseplay, camping around, and posing in life jackets, pretending to faint. Of the 885 male crew on *Titanic*, 693, or 78 percent, died. Altogether, 1,352 men perished. If, according to Kinsey, one out of six ordinary men is gay, 225 gay men died. If two out of six in the travel industry are gay, 450 gay men died, making *Titanic* an overlooked but essential chapter in gay history."

In the *Titanic* canon, and in the gay literary canon, the novel has won praise for its writing style, its precise accuracy in mixing fictional and historical characters, and its heritage as the first novel dealing with gay men on *Titanic*. Into this historic realism, Fritscher, writing in top erotic form, inserts the magical thinking of gay eros. You will never forget this story ripped from the secret pages of a *Titanic* diary!

Fritscher's fast-paced plot speeds along like a film. It has comic dialogue, high-drama queens, extremely able seamen, class-conscious sex, and the suspense of who will survive this story that begins like a musical comedy and ends with a sinking feeling. Fritscher looks through the prism of the *Titanic* microcosm to dramatize hidden gay history. It's an historical peek into how early twentieth-century gay folk, learning to save their own lives, helped invent modern homosexual identity, diversity, and politics.

Fans of gay subtext will appreciate that Fritscher wrote his parable *Titanic* at the height of the AIDS crisis when the speeding first-class party of the 1970s and 1980s, cruising on, crashed into the iceberg of HIV. How do gay people save themselves? Written in 1986 when only one or two LGBT book publishers existed, *Titanic* was first published in *Honcho* magazine (1988) where it was reader-tested as a serial novel nine years before James Cameron's *Titanic* (1997), and twenty-four years before Julian Fellowes of *Downton Abbey* filmed his *Titanic* (2012).

This tale of gay victims and gay survivors is historically accurate in its details of *Titanic* culture on board in all classes, and in its details of the ship, the sinking, and the rescue. Fritscher is also accurate in dramatizing quixotic gay psychology. Having been in the *avante garde* of literary erotica for nearly fifty years, and having won many awards, including a Lifetime Achievement Award from the Erotic Authors Association, he continues to refresh the genre. His remarkable tale of *Titanic* represents the new generation of gay fiction for the next generation of readers.

Mark Hemry
San Francisco, 2012

TITANIC!

Aboard *Titanic*. At sea. Westbound.
Wednesday, 10 April, 1912

Every night was a night to remember. The Astors had re-tired early from the grand first-class ballroom. So had the Rockefeller party. Edward Wedding, who was my lover since our second year at Oxford, sat next to me. He had excelled in sculling and sex while I, Michael Whitney, had distinguished myself with the British Romantic poets. And sex. Edward hated it when Mrs. Brown, who knew everything about everybody, teased him, calling him "Ever-Ready Eddy Weddy." She knew by looking, because Edward sported that certain look: the smug, engaging smile of a young man packing a big, how do you say in French, piece of pork.

Actually, we both had grown quite fond of Mrs. Brown who insisted she be called Molly. We three proved instantly agreeable tablemates the first day of the voyage as *Titanic* sailed proudly at noon from Southampton on April 10, Edward's twenty-sixth birthday. On *Titanic*'s brief stop at Queenstown, Ireland, Molly appreciated Edward's ship-rail comments about the hundreds of strapping young Irish tramping up the gangway to steerage, boys and girls immigrating to America's streets of gold. The shipboard gossip and salon *hauteur* was that Molly had been a showgirl, which was a scandal because showgirls, everyone knew, were always whores, no exceptions, thank you, even though Molly had married up into millions when she snagged the well-heeled land baron, the big-hung cowboy, Johnny Brown, back in Colorado.

Whatever she had been when she was on stage, Molly Brown was the kind of female who recognized two people in love, which, if it were two men, was aces by her. "Frankly, I prefer the company of you fellers. You know what you want when most don't. If love is what you got, you got more than the Astors. Besides, you dress better than the best, and you never laugh at any of my git-ups."

"Eddy Weddy," I said, "wants to wear your red ballgown with the red ostrich headdress." My American sense of sarcasm loved to pique Edward's British starch.

"Michael!" Edward said; no, Edward *commanded*. My dick stirred. His handsome jaw jutted out foursquare below his perfect white teeth and blond moustache. His eyes were bluer than the North Atlantic at high noon. His knee touched mine beneath the table. He had the strong body of a trained athlete. My cock rose thinking of his lean, hard thighs and long-muscled arms in his black cutaway. His tailor, lingering over measuring his long inseam, had commented how broad his sculling had made his shoulders, to say nothing, I mused, of his tight belly and mounded pecs, each crowned with a rosy brown nipple that grew hard when I sucked them and wet-rolled them between my fingers. His pecs and tits drove him crazy and made his big prick stand stalwart as a steel sword. As a coxswain to his crew, he was my cocksman in bed. "Michael," he repeated, "bugger off!"

Molly laughed in a tickling, tinkling cascade of feathers and diamonds and silk. This was our fifth night out, Sunday, on the magnificent ship. The eight-piece orchestra led swirling couples, colorful ladies held delicately by gentlemen in black, waltzing around and around the dance floor. "Everything smells so new," Molly said. "New wood. New paint. My new good fortune. And us new friends here, snug as bugs in a rug in the North Atlantic. I want it never to end!"

"Here, here." Edward said.

"All I want," Molly whispered, "is more ice in this fancy drink." She leered at Edward, waving her small hand, bejeweled with diamonds. "I simply adore big fat chunks of ice."

Four nights before, the very first night, Edward had asked our red-headed purser, Felix Jones, if rumor he had heard about the catwalks above and through the boiler rooms, and the hallways in the crew quarters in other ships was to be the case with *Titanic*.

"Cruising, you mean, sir?" Felix winked. "Why *Titanic*'s a cruise ship, isn't she now?"

"And the very fastest in the world," I said. "Top speed, 30 knots."

"Then," Felix said, "I suggest you young gentlemen head fast and quiet down the back stairs portside, say, about 11 o'clock. You'll find what you're looking for where the women never go. Some say first-class never mixes with second-class nor with steerage to say nothing of mixing after hours with the crew. What you see on your tickets, and what deck is your promenade, has no meaning below stairs. There's no distinctions down in the hold. Just men being men. Is there anything else I may do, gentlemen?" Felix was good-looking, a big-boned Welshman, no more than 22, our age, but we were reared worlds apart.

"Yes," Edward said. "Whom would you recommend?" He made a slow show of unbuttoning his shirt.

"Down below, sir?"

"Yes." He stripped off his shirt and stood magnificently buffed to the waist.

"I'm partial to the boiler-tenders, sir. The coal-heavers." The red-headed purser's face was flushing with sudden lust. "Shoveling coal night and day makes them strong."

"And dirty," I said.

"Which can be," Edward said, "a virtue."

"Why, Eddy," I said. I teased his aristocratic need for sexual slumming.

Felix was fully aroused and hardly at sixes and sevens about propriety in the suites he waited. His hard cock showed big in his black trousers. He was no small man, a good five-foot-ten, gifted with the body of his coal-miner father. He had worked in the mines of Wales as a boy and young man, and the work had made him strong. His tailored uniform could not disguise his deep-chest, tight biceps, moon rump, and thick thighs that left no room for his hardening cock to be decent in a first-class suite.

I could see in his green eyes the cautious, yet confident, look the lower classes have, because they know they're what the upper classes seek most when they slip out on the slum. In heaven or hell, or on the water, there's nothing more attractive to a rich man than a lower-class stud, even one bettering himself by choosing to be a purser rather than a shoveler in the boiler room. Felix Jones had had enough of coal in Wales. On the high seas, he had a taste for serving young gentlemen.

Edward took a step toward Felix, reached around him, locked the door, and groped his hand along the shiny length of the well-trained purser's untrained, hard cock. Felix's head rolled back on his strong neck. I unbuttoned his shirt and brushed my nose through the surprise of thick red hair covering his chest, licking into his sweat-sweet armpits, and tonguing his nipples.

Edward unbuttoned the man's trousers, springing out a 9-inch cock, the alabaster white kind twined with thick blue veins peculiar to translucent penises rooted in a thatch of hickory-red hair. We were all three quickly stripped naked as the Queen's Guard at bath call. Edward fell to his knees sucking Felix's thick shaft, no gagging or gurgling, merely smooth moves, sliding his face down on the purser's hard cock, as naturally as he had taken to the long oar in sculling on the Thames where I had only dared punt.

I stood on the bed and shoved my fat dick down the redhead's mouth, glorying in the sensation of his thick red moustache bristling, brushing my cock topside. With my hands, I played their four tits like a bumblebee concerto for twin pianos. Edward pumped his long, sleek, thoroughbred horsecock with his hand, the way he preferred to control his cuming, unless it was, as it had usually been from the start, shoved up my ass the way he'd first reamed my hole with his long rod the rainy Oxford afternoon we'd met at the foot of Christopher Wren's Tom Tower in the great quad of Christ Church.

His 10-inch cock for the first three months was 3 inches too big for me, and then, suddenly, he said he loved me, and my cheeks spread, my hole opened up, and he drove his 10 inches to the hilt deep into me. Light, blinding as dawn piercing a rose window, illuminated me from my asshole to my head. The best measure of any big cock's true length and width and volume is the measure a man makes of it clamped deep inside his butthole. Vlad the Impaler had nothing on Edward Wedding. "And I love you," I said.

Edward's forceful sucking was too much for Felix Jones who had never been throated so skillfully in all his life in

Wales. As he began to cum, he began to shout. He was really quite amusing. To silence him, I screwed my own cock down his face as far as I could thread my thick 8-inch piece of Boston pipe. My cum burst down so deep inside him, his shouting turned to moaning. Cum spurted from his nose and his mouth. His tongue licked clots of hot white seed from his red moustache, and his green eyes widened in a kind of awed gratitude. (I like to think.) The sight and feel of dripping cum and spit, mixed with my telling Felix to grab hold of Edward's tits and squeeze-roll them as tight as he could, caused my masturbating Edward to shoot the load from his 10-inch cannon all across the new rose carpet of *Titanic*.

Maniacs, we fell in a tangle, in a peerage of sex, upon one of the single beds, all three of us, equal, grown young men, in a sweaty pant, huffing and puffing, laughing and eating cum from fingers and chests and moustaches and flopping wet cocks. Edward was so jolly. He lifted Felix's perfect redhead's dick, its thickness in sausage proportion to its length.

"You, Felix, are truly titanic!"

He broke out three cigars and we lay abed, smoking peacefully, talking and cuddling, comparing cocks, and doing everything *encore*, on that our first night at sea as *Titanic* sped through the dark waters of the North Atlantic, toward America, toward New York, toward home.

"*Titanic*," Molly Brown asked. "What does it mean?"

"The Titans were rebellious gods who were too big for their britches," Edward said. "They wished to overturn the established order."

"Good for them," Molly said.

"I think rather," I said, "the ship is named for Titania."

"Who's she?" Molly asked. "Should I meet her?"

"She's the queen of the faeries," Edward said. "Shakespeare."

Edward was evening the score for my teasing him. "You already know her, but her name this time is Michael." He pointed at me.

"Then, Michael," Molly said, "I add you to the list of royalty of my recent acquaintance."

"Queen Michael," Edward said, working his vengeance on me for laughing at Molly's dubbing him "Eddy Weddy."

"Don't be ridiculous," I said. "No man should ever be called a queen."

"Some men should," Edward said.

Molly pealed with laughter. I'd have punched her, but she was a suffragette and I heard they punched back.

"May this then," Edward said, raising his glass in a champagne toast, "be the start of a great tradition." He grinned. "To Queen Michael!"

"I'll drink to that," Molly said. "To Queen Michael."

Decorum overcame my anger at the feminine suggestion. In America, I had worked since boyhood to make my gestures and voice as masculine as my body, and found in England less pressure for a comfortable compromise. "Ha!" I said, "Ah-ha!" I lifted my own glass. No better way to squelch a joke than to join it. "To Queen Michael," I said, "and don't you, my subjects, forget it." I snatched Molly's diamond tiara from her head and crowned myself. They all laughed.

"Keep it," Molly said. "That glass looks better on you than it does on me." "That glass" was twenty-two 10-carat Hapsburg diamonds. "Sooner or later everyone needs a tiara, my dear. You may need it someday." She put her hand on mine. "My sweet young man, let Molly bring you luck."

The second night out, promptly at 11, Felix led us down five flights of backstairs to the hold. The noise of the engines, only a purr in our stateroom, drowned out the sound way above of the orchestra playing the "Varsouviana." The roaring, revolving engines drove their long steel pistons deep into *Titanic*'s guts like huge copulation machines. The maze of catwalks was lined at both rails with sailors, coalmen, cooks, mechanics, and blackamoor masseurs from the Turkish steam room. The hot red tips of the crewmen's rolled cigarettes and the gentlemen's cigars blinked with each drag in the dark like stars signaling in the night. We threaded our way through the silent, standing men, taking our bearings.

"I leave you gentlemen here," Felix said. "They look rough. They are rough, most of them, some of them, no doubt, criminals, but they know where they are. *Titanic* is their discipline. They must be careful with nowhere to escape but the open sea. So you are safe. Perfect, yes? They know you are not them. The same as you gentlemen, they have their terms. They want at night only what they give you by day. Service." He turned, then turned back. "Enjoy yourselves, gentlemen." He disappeared through the lounging lines of men standing in the half-darkness of the red bulbs lighting the engine room.

"Let's take an adventure," Edward said. "Let's split up."

"Divide and conquer."

He put his arms around me, even surrounded as we were by so many dark eyes in the red glow. "I love you," he said.

"I love you," I said. "More than life itself."

"Ah," he said, "but not more than all this irresistible cock."

"Let's regroup at our suite."

"When?"

"Whenever."

"Our clock is not ticking."

"Time is not running out on us. We have a week to kill on this voyage."

We parted company and I cruised out on my own, slowly strolling down the catwalk, eyeing the sailors and laborers, growing bolder with each step, stopping, staring, eye-to-eye, measuring my choice. *Titanic* was like half of Noah's ark: there was one of every kind.

A hand pulled on my trousers. I looked down at a blond lad with the face of an orphaned angel. "Take me, sir. Only one quid."

"No one told me anyone charged by the 'pound' down below," I said.

"I do, sir."

He was a ragamuffin cabin boy. His confident smile told me he usually received what he asked for.

"All right then, first tell me how big you are."

"Fourteen, sir."

"Fourteen inches? My! My! Then you are worth something."

"No, sir. Fourteen years. Next month."

"Sorry, my boy. I'm looking for beef not chicken."

"I need the money for my sick mother back in Liverpool."

"You have the stench of an orphanage about you."

"Nossir. I mean, yessir, but I seen you above deck and you looked..."

"Like a mark."

"Yessir. You all look, forgive me, sir, like marks to a lad like me."

"Here." I laid a sovereign in his soft hand. "The money's for you, not your mother, isn't it?"

"Who else, sir? My mother's been dead long since I was born. Eighteen years ago."

Of legal age, but selling his wares as a "young boy," off he ran into the darkness. I wondered at the justice in the world where the B Deck middle-class was chained off at the stairs leading to first-class of A Deck, and steerage was caged off, lower down on C Deck, to keep them from reaching middle-class. *Titanic* was a true social microcosm. Ah, well, perhaps my small donation to the lad would bring me luck with a bruiser of a man.

I grew bolder. A sailor, blond-bearded, short and barrel-chested, stood insouciant against the rail, his white uniform bright in the dark. The flap of his trousers was unbuttoned. His huge cock hung an easy 8 inches soft against the down-turned flap. I walked up to him and touched his beautiful blond beard. He smiled and sucked my finger into his mouth with his hot wet tongue. I made love to his bristled face, raking his beard with my teeth, sucking it with my lips. I dropped one hand to his cock. The soft, foreskin-hooded, fat shaft began to rise hydraulically.

"Suck me," he said.

I looked left and right. Everywhere men were tangled up. No rules applied below deck. I fell to my knees, tonguing and lipping the tip of his cock.

"I said, *suck me.*" His voice rose deep from his big hairy balls.

I slid down his uncircumcised cock. He reached down and unbuttoned my shirt, feeling for my nipples. His slowly engorging cock hung soft as a long fat slug waiting for me to suck its 8 inches up to 10. Its skin was blond-baby soft, softer than velvet. It rolled to the left of his groin, hardening under my study. Alive. Pulsing. Its color in the red light was that fresh-meat pink peculiar to blond dicks. He flexed his tool like a muscle. It bounced and rolled. The cockhead peered like an eye from the circling lid of foreskin. He smelled clean enough, and nasty enough. I took his meat in my hand and licked my forefinger, inserting it inside his foreskin, circling its big mushroom head, feeling clots of cheese scoop ahead of my finger. I pulled out and looked at his smegma, an *hors d'oeuvre* sweeter than any first-class buffet could provide.

"You too good for that, sir?" Disdain tinted his voice.

"I, sir," deliberately throwing the term back to him to show him he was boss, "live for such delicacy."

"Then gi' me the pleasure to see you eat it."

The thick clot of blond cheese was tastier than Danish brie. I rolled it like a connoisseur on my tongue, sucked it through my teeth, wanting the taste of him in my mouth to linger strong when next I kissed Edward, himself out harvesting the juice of men for me.

"Show it to me on your tongue," he ordered.

I opened my mouth and held out my tongue. He smiled, and dropped a long, thick strand of spit directly from his mouth to mine.

"Mix it up and swallow the pud," he said. His cock was rising by degrees, like some leviathan from the dark sea. He enjoyed toying with men like me who like to be the toys of men like him.

I squished his cheese and spit, mixing it into a heaven-sent *paté*, Smacking my lips to please him.

"Swallow it," he said.

I savored one last taste and gulped his juices down my throat.

His cock stood at hard attention, its head still shrouded by its cowl of foreskin.

"Peel me back," he said. "With your tongue."

I worked my tongue across his big piss-slit and into his foreskin, finding more of his cheese, swallowing it, wrapping both my hands around his hard cock, pulling the skin of the shaft down, popping the huge mushroom head of his enormous cock free of the envelope of his foreskin.

"Suck me." He said it the way I'm sure he said it to Amsterdam whores. I could tell that his cock was the center of his blond, bearded, well-built being. He had the ruggedly handsome look of a man who always got what he wanted sexually.

With no trouble at all.

Especially from me. I took the bulbous head of his dick into my mouth. Its hard volume plugged my face. I worked his uncut head in and out. His fully stiff cock stood the length of my two handsful between my crossed eyes. He was a choker. He knew it. He liked it. My tongue fucked his piss-slit. He moaned. I bit lightly on his head. He moaned louder. I chewed the head of his cock. He slapped the side of my head with his calloused hand.

"Suck me," he commanded. "Go down on me." A litany of profanity spilled out. "Swallow my big hard blond cock all the way down your bloody throat till you feel the bloody hairs in my crotch scratch your bloody nose."

I obeyed. I took him inch by inch, swallowing, savoring slowly the masculine taste and soft skin of his strong cock.

"I said, *suck it!*" He liked fast, robust sucks. He put his giant hands on the back of my head, curled his tough fingers into my hair, and jammed me into a nose-dive down to the base of his steel rod. In and out, working his dick like the pistons ramming *Titanic* engines, battering my throat, tears watering from my eyes, spit and cockjuice drooling from my mouth, my nose foaming, my voice choked to groaning that grew louder the harder he fucked my face. His demands, commands, in abandon, turned to snarls and grunts. He plugged the O-ring at the back of my mouth, the final ring that leads down the throat, with his mushroom head. I whipped my own cock to a frenzy as he drove me, kneeling, and bent me over backwards, till he had lowered me flat to the catwalk and straddled me. Never once did his cock leave my face, even as he fell to his knees and, pumping push ups, drilled me deep, pulling almost out past my sucking, begging lips.

What a common uncommon sight we must have made! Feet and legs gathered in a circle three deep around us. Dark shadows of men stroking their cocks watched the wild show of his wild fuck of my face. His rams became stronger, faster, more urgent. The crotch flap of his whites whipped my chest, exciting my nipples. My cock was mine. He cared nothing about it juicing in my fist. I reached both my palms up to cup his perfect butt through his white sailor cloth, but he bucked my hands off, muttering, "My ass is mine! Eat my cock, you fucking cocksucker!"

Men, staying well out of the muscular blond sailor's way, fell to their knees in a circle around my head lying on the catwalk floor. Cocks of every size and shape shot their loads on my face. I was drowning in sperm. The more he fucked, the more shooting cocks replaced shooting cocks. My hair matted with anonymous cum. My throat ached with his ramming. My cock pitched to the breach of cuming. He lunged. He roared up his full height on his knees: his big wet dick, swung free from my mouth, red with heat, flailing in the air, searching like a lost ship for the port of my mouth. He swore. He cursed. He blasphemed. He took his raging dick in both his meathooks and plunged it one last time so far down my throat I feared his load might shoot out my ass. Again, he withdrew, this time a slow suctioning pump, sump-pumping himself up to his final blast, pulling his pole, inch by inch, from my mouth and kneeling across my chest, raising his arms out sideways from his muscular hips, crooked forward at the elbow, his hands fists, mighty above my face, and with a roar that started in his balls, shot up his spine, hit his head, shot again back down his spine to his balls, he exploded long aerial flumes of white sperm across my face, with me cuming in my own hand, my mouth open, swallowing, eating his load, eating the dozen other loads of men whose cocks he triggered by his big shoot.

Upstairs in the Main Salon, Molly Brown was dragging a reluctant table or two of reticent rich into a chorus of the popular "Meet Me in St. Louis, Louis." Edward was by her side. His evening had been fun, if not tame, and he had spent an hour with Madame Ouspenskaya whose unsettling reading of his Tarot he was trying to forget.

"I saw you," he said, in our stateroom. "You were disgusting."

"Yes," I said. "I know."

He grinned. "Let me lick all that cum from your face and your hair." He pulled out his hardening cock.

"And we still have three glorious nights to go before *Titanic* docks in New York."

One month after the sinking of *Titanic*, Molly Brown attended a
memorial ceremony in New York.

The *Titanic* Gymnasium
One of the *Titanic* engines

Aboard *Titanic*. At sea. Westbound.
Friday, 12 April, 1912

Travel heightens observation. One remembers details, impressions, feelings. The Ryersons spoke to the Astors and the Astors spoke only to God knows. Poor Molly Brown, dragged up in her feathers and boas with a fat purse bulging with new cash, couldn't truly jolly her way into that tightest of first circles. If it wasn't her clothes she tripped on, it was her brash sense of Colorado humor. "I'm just you before you married a bank account," she said to Mrs. Leland-Wynston. Maggie came on like a hatpin in a salon stuffed with balloons filled with hot air. The rich prefer to buy their jesters, safe clowns, not pointed wits like dear sweet Molly.

Edward and I escorted the redoubtable Mrs. Brown for a brisk walk on deck. The sea was calm. The stars were brighter than ever I'd seen.

"First-class is such a bore," Molly said. "No wonder you boys disappear early every evening leaving me alone with that little pack of Spanish gigolos. I swear they boarded with nothing but their Brilliantine hair tonic and their tuxedos with empty pockets hoping to earn their way by dancing horizontal tangos across the North Atlantic. By God! I've never paid for it. Although I have been paid."

"Why, Molly," Edward said. "How droll."

"Eddy Weddy," Molly stopped us dead in our tracks. "Do I for one minute look...*droll?*"

"Molly, you always look wonderful," I said.

"Thank you, kind sir." She patted her hourglass figure. "I have appeared on the stage," she said. "Make of that what you will. Everyone else seems to."

"I apologize," Edward said.

"Don't be an ass," Molly said. She took us both by the arm and like a decorated tugboat steered us toward the prow of the ship.

"The night is lovely." I tried to make conversation.

Two decks below us, a piano and concertinas and tin whistles rose in harmony with the gales of Irish laughter of the hundreds of passengers dancing and singing in steerage. We peered over the railing. The sight was sweet. Young couples held each other close. A young father danced with his two infant sons in his arms while his wife, all of them looking straight from County Cork, danced with him, her arms outstretched to his waist, circling in her family. The dance floor was circled by men waiting their turn to catch some idle girl. Even the homeliest would do. The men in steerage outnumbered the women six to one.

"So this is what the simple folk do," Edward said.

"Don't be a snob," Molly said. She turned an inquisitive glance on both Edward and me. "What do these men do?"

Edward and I broke into laughter.

"That's what I thought," Molly said. "Stop laughing and tell me. I left Colorado to find out everything about the world."

Needless to say, Molly got an earful, though Edward was too much the gentleman to distress her with certain facts, or worse, certain rumors. *Titanic,* some said, was built so fast by its construction crew, welding massive iron plates, driven to even speedier work by investors, that stories spread that laborers who lagged behind were welded up alive, abandoned and forgotten inside *Titanic*'s giant echoing bulkheads.

Edward, ever polite, delivered Molly the superficial truth, as glycerine-smooth as the waters of the North Atlantic sea spread so flat and calm as far as we could see. I, ever the literature scholar, could have told her the same tale, but more like Chaucer, deeper, "The Stoker's Tale," deep as the sea we skimmed across, deep as the dark hold was below the glimmering lights of the Grand Ballroom where the band played on, all of us pilgrims to Canterbury. Voyeur that I am, I had followed Edward down below deck. I knew how he was when he was with me. I wondered how he was with other men.

Edward's 10-inch cock drew men like magnets; but Edward, for all his aristocratic distinction, was fickle as everyone else. No matter how big one's own cock, the search is always for a man whose cock is bigger. "The hung don't care to fuck down." Edward had once said that.

"But I," I said, "have only 8. That's 1 inch for each of my 8 million bucks when daddy dies."

That made him laugh and grow tender. "But you I love," he said. "When I go slumming, that's a different story."

Love and slumming.

I spied the man even before Edward. I knew his taste for the heroic. The giant stood in the shadows, a coal-heaver, a stoker, stripped to the waist, his chest and shoulders as magnificent as his powerful arms. His face was the kind of rugged brute handsome that makes dicks rise. His tousled hair and short beard were black as the coal-grime covering him from head to foot. Even so, his nipples jutted prominent from his pectorals, nipples almost pink in the red lights of the hold, as if he had licked his dirty fingers and tweaked them clean. His hands, like his hairy forearms, were massive from heavy labor.

I could only guess, as could Edward, what all this upper-body promise meant below his carved waist, cinched tight with a rope holding up his coal-heaver's blackened leather pants. His big feet, spread wide in black boots, formed a tri-angle up to his crotch where the leather barely concealed the thickness of his long driving ram. He was an animal, born so, the kind of man rich men hire to power their empires, their factories, their ships.

He was, I sensed, the man who made *Titanic* go.

He waited as if he knew Edward was advancing toward him and him alone. He groped his huge crotch. He groaned deep from his big balls. His lips parted the dark thatch of his short, rugged beard. His white teeth shone, not in smile, but in heat. Men kept their distance. He towered well over 6-3 and weighed in at a hard-packed good 265. He was a Goliath, perfect for *Titanic*. Perfect for Edward. Actually, perfect for me. For the first time, I felt a fleeting, just fleeting, twinge of jealousy. It wasn't I didn't want Edward to have him. It was more I wanted him too, but that, as it turned out, was never to be.

Edward walked straight up within three paces of the Stoker. Each surveyed the other. Edward's hard, lean-muscled body looked good to me in the dim red light. He pulled off his shirt, exposing his sculler's chest and broad shoulders. The two men stood stripped to the waist, squared off, stanced like men who are about to make love like fighters. The Stoker raised both his massive arms, flexing them the way I had seen Mr. Sandow exhibit his biceps in a gentlemen's salon in London. Eugen Sandow, having set the fashion for physique posing, would have fled back to Germany had he seen the Stoker's arms, his sweaty armpits, and the twin mountains of his nipple-crowned chest. He lowered his challenging arms and stroked one hand across his hairy pectorals and down his sculpted hairy belly, stopping only when his big hand cupped his crotch.

Edward reached for his wallet and placed a hundred pound note on a box halfway between them.

The Stoker nudged a coal-heaver next to him who picked up the bill. "That's for what hardness you seen," the Stoker said. His accent was Czech, but his English was clear. "What else depends."

"Depends on what?" Edward, ever undaunted, was especially bold with a hardon.

"Depends on what you got." He groped his grimy crotch, bouncing his almost visible cock and balls. "Depends on what you want."

The surrounding coal-heavers and more than several slumming gentlemen laughed.

Like a gambler with an ace in the hole, Edward palmed his hard 10-inch cock, exhibiting its outline in his trousers.

The laughter stopped dead in the water.

Except for the Stoker. "I eat that for snack."

Edward was expert at fencing. He took a step forward, closing the distance between them, and parried. He pointed at the Stoker's crotch. "I eat that for another hundred pounds."

"Crazy rich Britisher boy," the Stoker said. "You will eat my whole focking body before you eat my big focking cock."

He raised his arm, exposing his wet armpit. I nearly swooned from the rich sweet smell of his body. Edward took the last step in. The Stoker took him with one hand on the back of his head and pushed his face into the sweaty, muscled tangle of long black hair. Edward, Molly's "Ever-ready Eddy Weddy," landed willingly, tongue-first in the Stoker's armpit. He made sucking, slurping sounds that made my cock hard.

I wasn't the first man, coal-heaver or gentleman, all equal voyeurs, who pulled my cock from my trousers to stroke along with their rugged foreplay. Edward and the Stoker stopped all the other action in the vicinity dead in its tracks, just like the couple on a dance floor who are so good all the other dancers stop in a sophisticated circle to watch and applaud. I knew Edward loved theatre, but I'd never known him to give a performance.

I knew we'd both remember this little show till the day we died.

The Stoker, with one strong hand, moved Edward from one armpit to the other, dragging his wet and willing tongue through the thick hair on his chest, hair matted like seaweed around the aureole islands of his big leather-tough nipples. His muscular arm bulged. Huge veins, heated with hard work and stoked with passion, coiled like snakes through the black hair furzing his biceps and hamhock forearm. No doubt his cock was even more thick-veined.

He guided Edward's sweaty blond moustache and licking tongue up to his dark beard. "Chew it! Eat it!"

Edward slurped the sweatsalt from the Stoker's coarse beard. Tight curly black hairs caught in his teeth. He chewed like the challenger he was and came at the coalman full force, following the dance, but never giving an inch. The tougher the Stoker got, the rougher Edward responded. I thought I could see in the Stoker's eyes a hint of dumb surprise. Few men, if any, ever gave him what he wanted much less upped the ante.

He yanked Edward back by the hair, held his head six inches from his face, and stared at him eye to eye, man to man, sizing up this startling young gentleman athlete the way Goliath must have looked at the young David standing defiant with a rock in his hand.

He spit, a long white flume of spit, into Edward's face.

Edward spit it back. And grinned.

The Stoker's breath was as sweet as when he had been a muscular boy harvesting the hay fields of Czechoslovakia. He was younger by ten years than his huge size made him look. With Edward's spit hanging like white cum in his black beard, he was no more than 30, but his command presence made him seem like an ancient god.

They stood frozen in the circle of masturbating cocks. The Stoker laughed, broke the *tableau*, and from his laughing mouth, in the distorted shadows of the red light, his tongue, long and tubular inched slowly from between his lips, the head of it, swear to God, looked in the brilliant darkness like nothing so much as the head of a Roman-orgy cock, the way the sides rolled up, forming a piss-slit, the shaft of it coming out hard as a dick, slow inch by slow inch, the blue veins stark, mean, the volume tumescent, sticking out big and hard, a cocklike blowgun bulleting out thick white clots of spit rapid as a Gatling gun, targeting Edward's open mouth, a foaming pool of the Stoker's sweet cumlike juice.

Edward, not to be outdone, spit the load back on the Stoker's greasy chest, white-hot lather mixing into the thick black hair forested across the big man's high, wide, and handsome pecs.

That did it.

The Stoker drove his 5-inch tongue, mushroom-head and shaft, straight through Edward's lips and deep into the back of his mouth, tongue-fucking him hard as any cock, hawking his spermy spit back into his throat, shooting the cum of his spit into Edward's guts.

All this presentation of credentials, two stags squared off, took all of six minutes. The rest took longer.

Edward rebelliously jerked his hair loose from the Stoker's grip. He popped open his trousers, dropped his shorts, and displayed his 10-inch rockhard cock. Three masturbating bystanders, two lords, and one lord who was a lady trapped in a lord's body, shot their loads on the spot. Edward wrapped both his hands, big-boned from rowing team, around his shaft, squeezing the angry purple head of his dick to plum-size. He grinned his challenge, then spit his own spit splat-down on the leather crotch of the Stoker's tentpoled pants.

The Stoker growled.

There was ass on the line.

The crowd howled.

The Stoker slowly unbuttoned his leathers. He teased a gruff tease like some primal folkdance. Anticipation in the circle of voyeurs grew. His hairy white thighs, untouched by coal-grime, glowed with sweat in the red light.

His dick was so long and so hard, it hung like a galvanized pipe three-quarters of the way down his thigh. The man was hung with a horsecock crossbred with bull balls. A groan, a sigh, and slight applause rose from the audience who'd given up betting for masturbating. It was obvious. Edward and the Stoker, two different classes of men, were as perfect an odds-on match as *Titanic* was for the North Atlantic.

"When I beat you, young gentleman, sir," the Stoker said. He appreciated Edward's cock and cockiness. "You will stay with me for 24 focking hours below decks in the hold, in the boiler room, maybe even in chains in the brig, just so you see, young gentleman, how men like you make men like us live."

Edward, ever the knightly aristocrat, picked up the gauntlet. He hated socialism and bolshevism; he took on the Stoker's dare as if the laborer were the devil Trotsky himself. As an American man, matched, mmm, "married," in great subtlety, to a bit of a British snob, I had to listen at tea to such lordly politics with feigned sympathy, when, I, like Molly Brown, much preferred the social leveling of the bedroom where everyone, Astor and Guggenheim, ends up horizontal, even as, I bet, Trotsky himself, with his legs in the air.

How could Edward not win for losing on the Stoker's dare? Edward either took the Stoker's 14-fat-inches down his throat, and, mind you, up his ass, or he had to spend a day and a night in the hold getting up to the Stoker's "focking" speed, outdistancing his old sculling records, the way *Titanic*, slicing through the still, cold waters was outdistancing itself and her sister ship, *Olympic*.

The Stoker stripped naked to his boots. Edward shucked his clothes and shoes. A sailor started rapping a rhythmic tattoo on the iron railing in time to the rods pistoning the huge engines. The Stoker was a stroker, wrapping both big hands around his cock, squeezing out a third handful, vein-popping the bulbous mushroom head, its piss-slit dripping translucent 40-weight lube webs. His was a savage cock, primitive, animal, evolved somehow, from the mountain giants of Eastern Europe into a steel-hard, mechanized piston. The way his ox-driving ancestors wielded their barbarian swords, the Stoker aimed his ram at Edward like some unspeakable industrial weapon.

I fairly swooned.

Lucky Eddy Weddy. Was he ever ready for this?

Oh, my, yes. The Stoker, I knew, was the stuff of Edward's dreams. No matter his politics.

No sooner did I take my own hard cock in my hand than a handsome young sailor, blond as Melville's angelic Billy Budd, dived mouth-first on it, freeing me to grope the cocks standing hard out all about us, every eye fixed on the Stoker, double-fisting his animal cock. Edward, who knelt only to royalty, recognized the regal superiority of the noble savage, and fell to his knees, his own 10-inch cock stiff enough to fly the colors, his mouth open as wide as a choir boy stuck on the jaw-dropping fourth note of "Oh, Holy Night."

The Stoker roared.

The crowd roared.

Titanic roared.

I feared for Edward's life and limb, but I knew he'd die a happy death with his limbs all over the place. Slowly, savoring his dripping gusto, the Stoker drove the full circumference of his dickhead into Edward's open mouth, hungry for the only thing he had ever hungered for in all his privileged life. First-class dining was not upstairs. Downstairs, real life teemed.

The Stoker's roar caused two men boxing hardon-naked fifty feet away to stop their bare-knuckle fisticuffs.

Edward ate the apple-sized dickhead like Adam swallowing in Eden. He dropped his jaw, fearful of scraping the giant's meat. The Stoker's hairy body flexed, driving his fist-dick in short, quick jabs and longer punches deeper into Edward's salivating mouth. Spit and sweat and lube dripped shiny down Edward's fine pectorals and belly. He put his hands on the Stoker's huge thighs.

"You like my focking, uh?" He finger-locked his thick hands around Edward's head, hands so big I could see only Edward's nose and his straining mouth as the Stoker drove inch upon inch of his battering ram, in, into Edward, always in, never pulling back an inch, choke-fucking his face, pulling finally back, pumping in and out, teasing open the back of Edward's mouth, the top of the tunnel of his throat, the hot, wet, tight throat where the Stoker aimed to plant the root of his cock that no man had ever swallowed whole before.

If a man has moments, Edward, I knew, kneeling between the grimy Stoker's legs, was having a night to remember all his life. My own cock was so close to cuming, I pulled the blond sailor off my dick and set him to work on my balls. Almost instantly, that triggered him. He rose up, a handsome devil, brandishing his long, hard cock, and shot ropes of white sperm up my belly. As soon as he came, he was gone. Another sailor dived on my dick. I guided him to my nuts. Other hands, other tongues licked cum from my torso. In the hot sea of sex surging about me, I thanked God I was tall. I wanted to be head and shoulders above them all so not to lose the vision of the Stoker's dick, obscenely white against his coal-skin, pistoning Edward's mouth. Edward always swallowed my 8-inches easily, and the Stoker had an easy 8 inches snaked down his throat. Edward, ever the sexual athlete, ever wanting *more*, was face-to-face with *more*. The Stoker had plumbed his throat with his first 8-inches and had 6 inches more of thick, hard cock to drive home.

I thought to call a halt, but in the dark night of the hold, the fires blazing in the furnaces, I knew what would seem in first-class as brutality was in truth the intense engagement of two men locked in sexual ritual older than prehistory, older than the gods, older than the Titans themselves. Besides, Edward was a strong, athletic sportsman who knew how to handle himself. He hardly needed me to climb through the invisible ropes of the invisible ring to referee a stop to the match.

For a moment, I saw his eyes, staring, between the Stoker's arms, down the fat 6-inch tube of remaining cock, determined to bury his nose in the muscular giant's curling crotch hair or die trying. Something, a lightning, as much lust as courage, flashed in his eyes. He gulped. The Stoker, not insensitive, drove a 9th inch slowly down into Edward.

Something clicked between them.

The Stoker seemed suddenly almost tender. More than he wanted to "fock" Edward by storm, he wanted someone to finally, really, totally swallow his 14-inch cock, to set an all-time land-sea record. Perhaps he sensed in Edward's willingness his chance, at last, to feel teeth and lips, chewing and sucking, at the big base of his cockroot. He oozed the 10th iron-hard inch down.

The crowd called out for more. A chant rose up. Pipes banged rhythmically. Money changed hands. Cocks rose up. Men shouted. Cuming. Sucking. Fucking. Watching. Shooting.

The Stoker and Edward both, a pair now, rose to the moment. I think Edward's throat actually opened an inch farther and literally suctioned the Stoker's 11th inch in so fast, the facefucker was jolted almost out of his big boots with surprise.

Edward had taken the offensive.

A grin broke through the Stoker's brute-handsome face. He had that space between his two solid front teeth that I've often found to be characteristic of truly aggressive sexual men. He took hardon pleasure in Edward's attack and sworded the challenge of his 12th inch, a foot of cock, down Edward's throat. It all happened so slow, so easy, almost so delicately, that I hardly noticed that Edward, whose goal in life had long been 12 inches, had swooned, fainted, passed out. Smiling in victory.

What to do? I pushed the suckers and lickers away from my cock and balls and tits and asshole. The crowd was too thick for me to make it the five feet to Edward impaled, hanging, jaw ajut, on the huge steel-hard cock. I shouldn't have worried. Felix Jones, our red-headed purser, had told us no harm could happen below decks. The Stoker himself, like the coal boss he was, flexed his massive body, establishing his command presence, and, like a conqueror barbarian, lifted Edward gently up, suctioning his dick out of Edward's throat, vacuuming up, popping finally the deep probe of his cockhead from Edward's grinning lips. His eyes fluttered open.

"Am I dead?" he asked.

"Not yet," the Stoker said.

"Good," Edward said. He spoke like a drunk happy on champagne. "We have another 2 inches to go."

"Focker!" the Stoker said. "But we reverse engines."

Bodily, he lifted Edward like a doll in his big-muscled arms above his head. His huge cock staffed its full 14 inches straight up 80-degrees dead ahead. Without so much as a quiver in his massive shoulders and chest and legs, he held Edward, his big hands in his armpits, his gnarled thumbs on his lean chest, like a conquered toy soldier above his head. The Stoker's cock drooled shine. His dick was a bulkhead as magnificent as *Titanic*'s jutting straight up, so erect its very skin stretched paper-thin over its ropes of veins and sinew. The tip of his cockhead, poised, waiting, drooling, dripping, flexing, like a ram awaiting its target to come bulls-eye to it.

I didn't need Mr. Muybridge to get the picture.

The still *tableau* of this *pas de deux* froze in the red-dark of the hold for an eternity of seconds. The crowd fell back, then forward, a hundred hard cocks masturbating at the sight, shooting up at them like flares in the night signaling the collision as the Stoker, slowly lowered Edward, ass-first, down through the arc of distance to the ice-hard head of his steaming cock.

The Stoker guided Edward's tight butthole straight down his slippery dick, its head popping the rim of Edward's skilled ass-ring, snaking, serpentine, deeper into Edward's ass, both of them roaring, each man making a match for the other, two animals locked in heat, flames from the belching furnaces lighting them, fucking like demons in the hot bowels of Hades.

The Stoker's steady cock was 7, then 8, then 9 inches plumb-deep in Edward's trembling body as their faces passed, longitude and latitude. The Stoker held Edward eye-to-eye.

"I fock you now."

"Fock me!" A beast inside my civilized Edward shouted.

A large bead of envy surged to the head of my engorged cock. Never had I conjured such lust in him; but my heart was glad he had found it in his daring self.

The Stoker, sweat running rivers from his armpits, grunted. His square teeth, separate as short pickets, grinned.

Edward grinned back. "Fock me!"

The Stoker spit a flume as white as cum.

Edward's face dripped. "Fock me!"

The Stoker slipped his big hands up Edward's raised arms, dropping him down on the 14-inch ram of his cock. Fully impaled, Edward roared with the beginning of satisfaction. He felt the Stoker's thick length stuffed deep inside him. His own 10-inch cock poled up from the valley where his thighs wrapped around the Stoker's muscle-narrowed waist. The penetration was complete. What was left was the "focking."

The Stoker stomped his boots, and the crowd fell back, as he carried Edward ten paces to the smooth iron cover of a throbbing engine. He eased Edward's torso down flat, pulling his rod of cock out to the neck beneath its inflated head locked inside Edward's ass-ring. They were poised against one another, with one another, in some inevitable destiny. The rhythms of *Titanic*'s mighty engines became theirs as the Stoker, slowly, then faster, began pistoning Edward's butt, driving in, drawing out, pounding in, tearing out, working together, rearing nearly apart, Edward's shouts almost as loud as the Stoker's grunts, coming harder, deeper, faster, his dick plunging to its massive root up Edward's ass, his bull-balls slam-banging into the iron engine cover.

The Stoker raised his huge arms, spread from his wide shoulders and massive hairy pecs, above his head, a triumphant victor, his hips and butt, planted firm on his booted thick legs, ramming, in rhythm to the engines, ramming his cock full-depth charge into Edward, pulling out all the way, ramming its big head again and again through the target of Edward's willing, dripping, hungry ass.

Again, they froze. They glazed over, the two of them, in the heat. The Stoker's cock was buried in Edward to the hilt. His upraised arms flexed, thick with power, the way his dick was flexing inside Edward's flexing ass.

The crowd sensed it. I knew it. The Stoker started a mighty roar. His muscular arms raised, his body fully flexed, he rammed Edward once more, held steady course deep inside him, and, fast as a flame leaps from a furnace, yanked his cock free. Posed in triumphant victory, he leaned in over Edward, laying the base pipe of his 14-inch cock topside over Edward's 10 inches.

Handless, he came.

Handless, his enormous cock shot wave upon crashing wave of white cum breaking across the shore of Edward's belly and chest and throat and face.

Handless, untouched, Edward's cock came, shooting up on the triumphant muscleman of a Stoker, hitting his hairy pectorals, creaming his belly, his rockhard, still sperming dick.

I came.

The crowd of men came.

The Stoker picked Edward up in his arms, carrying him, one forearm under Edward's knees, the other under his shoulders. His big cock, relentless, protruded hard from beneath Edward's forward buttock. Edward's own cock stood erect.

"I fock you," the Stoker said. "Now you lay the night with me."

Edward, my Edward, looked up at the Stoker, grinned, threw his arm around the giant's shoulder, and laid his cheek on the Stoker's grimy, hairy chest.

And off the Stoker carried him.

Perhaps Edward should have listened to Madame Ouspenskaya's card reading, foretelling danger, because events larger than our most fearful dreams loomed ahead, as *Titanic*, built for 24-28 knots, sped, at her captain's vanity, through the icy dark of the North Atlantic at a world-record 30 knots per hour.

Aboard *Titanic*. At sea. Westbound.
Sunday, 14 April, 1912

In the salons and smoking rooms, men toasted rumors of a record crossing. Twenty-four of *Titanic*'s 30 boilers were in service with preparations underway to light the remaining boilers for the next day's speed test. Edward was too exhausted from his night with the Stoker to accompany me to Sunday services convened in the first-class dining saloon. "Out of 2,000 passengers," Edward had gloated, "that coal-heaving Stoker chose me." Captain Smith read the service not from the *Book of Common Prayer*, but from the White Star Line's own prayer book. Shortly after 11 AM, with the ship's orchestra halfway through "O God, Our Help in Ages Past," I excused myself with a wink to the indomitable Molly Brown seated by my side. Even at service, Molly, dragged out in all her flamboyant finery, stood out like a bright yellow satin flower among the proper Astors and Vanderbilts and Ryersons attired in their subdued churchgoing blues, browns, and blacks.

"Go get 'em, sailor," she said.

I excused myself past the Thayers, the Carters, and President Taft's traveling aide Major Archibald Butt, who himself, I sensed, could hardly wait to adjourn to the fashionable *à la carte* restaurant where the George D. Wideners were to host an elegant party breakfast. Outside, near the Marconi Wireless Telegraph room, where operators Bride and Phillips were hard at work transmitting ship's messages as well as passenger messages to intermediary vessels for relay to London and

New York, I met Felix Jones, our red-headed purser who had provided so much frolic our first night at sea. His 8-inches were basketed discreetly in his tailored uniform. He grinned, without a word, and whisked me away for a surprise he had promised. In the wake of our leaving, Bride and Phillips must have exchanged the knowing glances of the straight-arrow. I heard their laughter and was not amused.

"Some men," I said to Felix, "just don't get it."

Bride and Phillips turned back to their messages.

"To *Titanic* and eastbound ships:
Ice report in latitude 42 N, to 41.25 N,
longitude 49 W, to 50.30 W.
Saw much heavy pack ice and great number
large bergs. Also field ice.
Weather good, clear."

Waiting for me in a well-appointed, but unoccupied second-class suite apparently reserved for discreet rendezvous, were the ship's second carpenter, Michael Brice, and Third Officer, Samuel Maxwell, both stripped naked, sitting in opposite Morris chairs, milking separate hardons, awaiting a Sunday service of their own.

"Gentlemen," Felix said, "may I present Mr. Michael Whitney."

Brice stood, cock jutting. Maxwell remained seated, cock rampant between his spread thighs. Felix, ever the gentleman's gentleman, discreetly withdrew. Not one word was spoken. Brice locked the door. I stripped. Resonant as a deep bass drum, *Titanic*'s engines hummed beneath the light slip-slap of Max's hand spit-stroking his big 9-inch cock. He was a solid, good-looking 38, better built than most officers. His neatly trimmed beard sported a becoming streak of gray. He exuded the confidence of a man whose logged nautical miles combined would have taken him around the world a hundred times. Brice had shipped out with him more than once. They had an understanding. Their relationship was pure lust. They rarely spoke. Their common interest, on long trans-Atlantic crossings, no more than the sexual gymnastics they staged together.

They liked to facefuck.

Double facefuck.

Cock to cock.

Both their dicks sliding together down one throat.

The rugged carpenter Brice and the commanding officer Max. Brice, blond and thick. Max, dark and regal. Brice, of almost equal age, 34 or so, both of them older men than I at 22. Brice with 9 inches moved toward me. My own 8 inches rose like a hard knot. Brice's tool-hardened hand clamped my shoulder, guiding me like a good boy down on my knees.

When my knees fold, my mouth opens. Some men like that in a man.

Brice did. He was no talk, all moves. He spit into the palm of his hand and spit-shined the big head of his cock, stalking on his big legs toward me, his fat prick aimed for docking in the open port of my waiting mouth. His coarsened carpenter's hand had calloused his carpenter's cockhead. Its pink skin, worn rough, felt like the smoothest of fine sandpaper in my mouth. If ever a man were meant to "polish my sharp tongue down a notch," as my father had said when he shipped me off to Oxford, it was not my British tutors, it was Brice.

He worked my sucking lips and probed my mouth, driving left and right, tunneling for maximum headroom, surveying with his rod the drop he'd clicked down into my lower jaw, like a miner opening a cave wide enough for heavy machinery, to fit his cock inside up tight against Max's dick. Max! Who liked to deep-six his long, lean shaft down voyager's throats while Brice alternately plugged left cheek, right cheek, waltzing matilda, one, two, three.

A pair of lip-rippers they were, but my cock was up for the stretch even if my mouth had doubts. If Edward had taken the Stoker's 14 inches up his ass, my mouth could swallow the 18-inch double facefuck I saw coming. If not, by the time we docked in New York, I'd regret forever falling short of my lover's titanic feat.

I sucked a mouthful of Brice's globular head, wrapping my lips tight around the underlip of the corona. I felt I was swallowing one of Mr. Edison's electric bulbs: hot, large, and hard. I moaned. Behind the head of his slow-probing prow, my eyes, almost crossed, looked down the veined length of his sturdy, studhorse cock. He drove me over half-backwards. My hands left my cock to support me from behind. My head tilted up flat as a plate. His cock angled like a lever forging open my lips a crack, a crack wide enough for Max, moving slowly, cruising into view over my forehead, cock first, with a crystal glass in his hand.

He poured at least three fingers of absinthe over the hot head of Brice's cock, three fingers of 68% alcohol that I gulped without resistance down my throat. They knew what they were doing. My teeth retracted. My jaw dropped. My throat opened to a tunnel of fire. My head went absent without leave, absinthe without leave, I say now, and I fell into my sexual essence: I was no less than an open mouth with a hard cock kneeling before 18 inches of dick backed with enough male authority to rouse me to a fevered, perverted pitch, hungry, starving for the facefuck of the seedbearers, who, dickhead to dickhead, came v-shaped from left and right to rape my willing mouth.

Edward once had worked his sculler's fist all the way into my mouth and my passion for him had let me take the pleasure of his hard-knuckled fullness, my teeth wrapped tight around his thick wrist. My shipboard lust was no less for this anonymous pair of silent, brooding, insistent seamen. I was no more than a nine-hour virgin, having shot my load the night before watching the Stoker fuck Edward, but that was five hours more than I needed to reload fully, especially fueled by the sight of their big bodies, pronged with their pair of absinthe-slick dicks, closing in on me.

All the giddiness of Edward dubbing me "Queen Michael" and Molly crowning me with her embarrassing Hapsburg tiara was forgotten in the serious business at hand.

I had cock to suck.

I thought.

But I was wrong.

Brice and Max weren't seeking sucking.

They were fuckers, face-fuckers.

I was their face.

I was incidental.

Their unspoken-lovers' game was feeling their two dicks rubbing together, slip-sliding in and out, each revolving around the other, the way two athletic men clasp sweaty gladiatorial hands, gripping fists, intensely face to face, in the kind of pub arm-wrestling so popular throughout Britain, so scorned at Cambridge, so practiced at Oxford—arm wrestling introduced by the Romans centuries before. Never had I wanted to be a stranger in the world. Edward loved my American sense of exploration, and Brice and Max were new territory I took to with no map but my hard cock.

The two seamen got a high-speed, top-knot run for their money. I was every inch as much a cocksucker as they were face-fuckers. Edward had said he loved me because I was never passive, always active, even with his 10-inch oar rowing my deep ass. Brice and Max got the same treatment. I clicked my jaw down another notch and suctioned both their cocks into my mouth, holding them both hardon in my stuffed cheeks. They fucked together. Their side-by-side dicks alternately chugged my cheeks. Two man-size cocks, shipmates, buddies, silent lovers never speaking their own names, dick-to-dick, shaft-sliding slick, neck and neck, their matched 9-inch naval "short arms," fisted at the top with almost twin heads, wrestling cock-to-cock for advantage in the fighting arena of my mouth. What a bout! What a scrap!

My mouth felt like a writhing snake pit inside a boxer's punching bag.

In tandem, they slow-jabbed my face, Brice pummeling my cheeks, Max driving deeper, outdistancing Brice, his cockhead jamming the back of my mouth, stretching open the O-ring to my throat, pulling back behind Brice, taking my left cheek away from him, forcing him to my right cheek, their rods crossed like duellists' swords across my flat tongue, Brice fighting back, both cocks, competing, head next to head, stuffing my left cheek, ramming together, foaming my salivating mouth with their dripping cock slits, the licorice-sweet absinthe running deep fire down my throat, hungry for the depth-plunge, eager for the cheek joust, lusting for their combined 18 inches working my face, half expecting their cockheads to ram through the smooth plate of both my cheeks, crisscrossed cocks, smooth cheeks, gaping mouth, startled eyes.

That image of penis-rampant clicked in the back of my

head as the perfect family crest my straightlaced Boston Brahmin father deserved! The face of his wide-eyed, wide-mouthed son, with 18 inches of cock jutting triumphant from his cheeks, mounted on the mansion trophy wall like some strange-horned mythical beast hunted and killed by ancient ancestors. What a jape on my father who had never in his life even spoken the word *penis!*

A thought is but an instant in sex. Perhaps fantasy triggered by hardon reality is all of sex. The truth is the double entry of Brice and Max was the calm before the storm. Their cocks, colliding with my cheeks, forged hot in their foreplay. Together, they pulled out, popping my lips, my jaw hanging open, my tongue drooling ropes of absinthe spit to the twin heads of their dicks. Brice grabbed my hair to hold my head steady. Max delicately drove two fingers up my nostrils, tilting my head into place. My mouth, gasping for breath, hung like an open and willing target already on fire, burning like a boiler stoked by their sex-shovels. The three of us hung poised and ready. Brice spit down on his sandpaper dickhead and rammed me first, churning up my cheeks, his hand gripping my hair, Max's fingers stuffing my nose. I was foaming like a mad dog in the noonday sun, loving it, knowing who I was, not knowing what I was, my mind reeling mixed metaphors my professors would have shamed me for, but here was no shame, not in this sporting frolic. *Titanic* was a dreamship come true, a phantasm of imagination made so real only a fool could not actualize realities larger than his wildest fantasies.

Max tilted my nose left and right. Brice plunged right and left, calling for more absinthe. Max poured the hot liqueur straight from the bottle on Brice's cock. I gulped the churning foam, sinking beneath the battering ram of cock. Max pulled my nose up, gently. My eyes opened wide. The length of his huge dick spanned across my face, forehead to chin, its head red, slick, and dripping. Blue veins, thick as snakes, coiled tight around the log of his thick shaft. Brice held steady, docked in my right cheek. Max's face grinned way above his cock which loomed larger, closer than his head. He held my nose in place. Quiet settled on the three of us frozen in place like competing athletes waiting for the starter's gun. Sure as shooting, Max, driving his hard ramrod, pumping it in slow tattoo against my face, teased open my lips locked down on Brice's cock, slipping down alongside the length of carpenter cock, never hesitating, his cockhead, driven by his shaft, sliding across my tongue, snaking inch by inch to the back of my throat, docking with the O-ring, touching, teasing the membrane, readying to screw my head on to my shoulders.

He pulled his fingers slowly from my nostrils as he slowly drove his cock down my throat. He gave my breath back and took it away. Nose then mouth. Controlled breathing. Perfect moves. What could have been barbaric was athletic, even dancelike. I wanted Max and Brice. On their terms. They had won me over, conquered me. They stuffed my mouth and throat with too much cock for me to suck. My face was an open hole, a berth, home port, safe harbor. We were in delicate waters. I surrendered to their double-fuck.

Max slithered down my gullet, inching down, inching out, then down again, his fullness each time gaining deeper purchase on my throat, impaling me with hard cock, Brice, slow-pumping my cheeks, twin engines, working up full steam, easing me new into their accustomed fuck, timing themselves, jab, slip, slide, dip, ram, building the volume of cock, building the pace of fuck, slick they were, slicking themselves into me, chugging up their pace, throttling their alternating pistoning moves, their hard cocks stiffening harder side by side, two dick-buddies, fucking one face.

I've never yet met a man who, falling to his knees, did not wish his best friends could see him at that moment, some gasping in shocked horror, some applauding in envy. Going down is always the best revenge. On everyone. Even God.

Together they weighed more than a solid-built 300 pounds of force, irresistible, driving their tag-team cocks into my mouth. Max was rooted *basso profundo* deep in my throat strumming chords on my vocal cords. Brice took the treble clef jamming my cheeks *staccato*. Would that Edward had seen the operatic spectacle of our trio swaying in gathered fuck rhythm, building toward horned climax. Brice grunted more than Max and Brice's grunts directed the pace of their duet. His cock was swelling larger in my mouth, pulsing, throbbing alongside Max's iron rod. Cock-taste is like no other taste: sweaty, salty, sweet, and dirty. We fucked in perfect, rugged harmony. Upstairs, the band played on. Downstairs, the pair of seamen, carpenter and captain, force-fed their matched cocks. Brice was first to pass his limit: his fuck-speed picked up 10 knots, his grunts grew lower, tenser, his cock a battering gun pummeling my cheeks.

Max was not far behind. He put one muscular arm around Brice's broad shoulders and pulled him in close, poising him for the strike, ramming Brice's cock as much into his own hard shaft as into my cheeks. With a roar, Brice reared his head back, then whipped his face forward, staring down at the sight of his pumping cock double-fucking my face. He shot hard bullets of hot clot, filling my cheeks, ramming me, sliding alongside Max, his massive cock driving past his explosions, cocks colliding, driving Max deeper, the taste and smell of his seed boiling down my throat alongside Max's descending, pumping rod.

Max himself began a low groan in his big nuts. My throat opened and, rebellious fallen angel that I am, I swallowed him in deeper, taking half the head of Brice's dick along. Max twisted, stared hard down at my face, and, to reward me or discipline me, I have never known, drove his cock, shaft-fast past Brice's cock, and buried himself deep down, Brice holding my head by my hair. Max, profane as a parrot, cursed like a sailor, ramming his pulsing dick in place, shooting his depth-charge of white fluming sperm, exploding hot snot in my guts, down my throat, up out my nose, huge tidal waves of their mixed cum flooding from my lips, their two dicks, twisting hard, fighting for space, me choking, them panting, their big stiff pricks, held tight in place, forcing me to swallow, their fingers re-feeding me the cum escaping my lips, their draining dicks slowly, ever so slowly softening down to two fat snakes nesting in my mouth, licking them, sucking up their cum, them suctioning their twin 9-inchers from my face. When they saw I had cum without touching myself, they laughed, pulled me to my feet, and dropped me gently to the carpet. *Titanic* hummed along the full length of my backside as we sped together, fuck buddies, across the North Atlantic.

Edward thought my "Sunday picnic" was "ever so jolly." He said, "I rendezvous again with the Stoker. Tonight at 10. He wants to lock me in a cell in the brig, break in, and take me by force."

"Be careful," I said. "Remember Madame Ouspenskaya's Tarot reading."

"Don't be ridiculous," Edward said. "She's no mystic. She's no more than a nanny babysitting that Egyptian mummy Lord Ashcroft is sending to the New York Museum."

"That *cursed* Egyptian mummy," I said.

"Poo," Molly said at supper. "Of course, the mummy's cursed. No one pays admission if there's no curse. That's the thrill."

"That's one kind of thrill," I said.

Edward winked at Molly and they laughed uproariously. John Jacob Astor stared straight ahead.

At 9:30 exactly, Edward looked at his gold pocket watch, and excused himself from Molly and me, and our jolly party, in the Main Salon. Edward whispered, "He said he'd lock me up and throw away the key!"

At 10 exactly, stripped naked, his 10 inches hard in front of him, Edward found himself kneeling, locked in a cell, sucking the muscular Stoker's massive 14-inch cock through the steel bars. At 10:30, Edward, jacking his own cock, was ordered by the Stoker to back down and lie on the floor of the cell. The Stoker, as lead coalman, left to check on his boiler crew. Edward, disobediently, aristocratically, abandoning the common seaman's order to lie on the cold floor, lay alone on the single bunk in the cell, his cock in his hand, a smile on his face.

"I'm chilly," Molly said.

"I am always chilled," Madame Ouspenskaya stated.

Our table laughed. Even Mrs. J. J. Astor.

"Indeed," said the famous mystery writer Jacques Futrelle, who six days previous had celebrated his 37th birthday at a fashionable London restaurant. "An American gentleman told my wife that Captain Maxwell told him that between 7 and 10 PM the air temperature has dropped from 43 to 32 degrees."

"The promenade deck," Mrs. Futrelle said, "was noticeably cool this afternoon."

"Still," Madame Ouspenskaya said, "the sea is calm."

"There is no moon," Molly said wistfully.

"But the stars," I said, "shine brightly."

"Not as brightly as my diamond Hapsburg tiara," Molly said. She leaned her bosom close to me. "I hope you've stored it safely in the ship's vault."

"Actually," I said, "it's in our suite."

"You're as careless as me," she said. "No wonder I like you."

At 11:40, half our table looked up. The other half kept laughing, talking animatedly above the lustrous eight-man orchestra directed by bandmaster Hartley.

"What was that?" Molly asked.

"It sounded," Madame Ouspenskaya intoned, "as if a finger were drawn against the side of the ship."

The look on her face made my temperature drop faster than the evening air. At 21 knots, *Titanic* sped through the water at 300 feet in less than 10 seconds. "It has to be nothing," I said. "Look. Nothing has changed. The dancers. The music. The ballroom."

Molly agreed. "You fellas and gals should feel the earthquakes in Colorado."

In the Grand Ballroom there was absolutely no sense of shock. Below decks, deep inside the ship, in Boiler Room 6, on the starboard side, the Stoker heard the impact's crunching, and then a sound like thunder rolling toward him. A line of water was pouring through a thin gash in the ship's side two feet above the stokehole floor. He ordered his coal gang fast up the boiler room's emergency ladder.

Edward, pounding his pud, locked solitary two decks above in the brig cell, felt nothing but the shuddering of his own passion.

Below decks, watertight doors slammed closed amid the

raucous shrill of the alarm bells activated by First Officer William Murdock on the bridge.

In the postal sorting room on G Deck, the clerks began their hasty removal of mail to the higher decks. The elevators were not working, but the lights remained on without a flicker.

"Assess the damage," Captain Edward Smith ordered. To his dismay, at midnight, as Sunday, 14 April, became Monday, 15 April, he found that no more than twelve square feet of *Titanic* had been breached, but those twelve feet stretched, in a tear 3 inches wide, 300 feet along the ship's length, flooding five compartments. The ship could float with even the first four compartments flooded; but she could not survive the breaching of the fifth. "Had we but a moon," the Captain said, "we might have seen the face of the berg." Well he might have said, "Had we but a moon, we might have seen the face of God."

At 12:15, the Marconi Wireless room sent *Titanic's* first distress signals. Twenty-one-year-old Robert Hallam, wireless operator on the eastbound *Carpathia*, 58 miles south of *Titanic's* position, was stripping for bed, sleepily touching his penis, and about to turn off his receiver for the night, when he caught the call. *Carpathia's* Captain wheeled his course around making his slow, careful way through the ice fields of the open sea.

"I believe we've stopped," I said.

Still nothing changed. Through the Grand Ballroom window, I could see into the first-class dining rooms. Stewards were putting the finishing touches on the breakfast table settings.

Molly kicked one high-buttoned shoe up on the white linen table cloth. "My feet are still dry!" She made everyone laugh, but our laughter, our laughter—that had changed.

By 12:30, Thayers, Astors, Wideners, Ryersons, husbands, wives, families, accustomed to giving orders, not taking them, assembled on A Deck's forward side. The band stood on deck playing popular songs from operetta and the musical stage, and even the new sensation, ragtime.

I was frantic to find Edward.

Titanic was built to accommodate 2,435 passengers and 860 crew, a total of 3,295. On her maiden voyage, she carried 2,228 with 14 lifeboats and collapsibles; capacity: 980. At first, the boats were half-full, occupants boarding reluctantly, as much ashamed of doubting *Titanic*'s vaunted unsinkable reputation as they were afraid of the cold open sea at night. Exploding distress flairs rocketed like fireworks through the night sky. Near panic ensued.

"Women and children first!"

"It was a woman," I said, "who thought up that line."

"Women," Molly Brown said, "have always outsmarted men."

Portside, the more crowded side, only females and children were allowed in the boats by the crew armed with guns. Starboard, men could board if no women were present. Had we stupid cattle known then what we knew only later!

I saw no coalmen from below decks. If anyone could bring my Edward back up safe, it was the Stoker.

When 13-year-old heir Jack Ryerson was prevented by the loading officer from accompanying his mother, millionaire John Jacob Astor placed a woman's hat on the young man's head and pronouced, "So, now, you're a girl and you may go."

Molly's eyes lit up.

"I must find Edward," I said.

"Edward," Molly said, "knows how to take care of

himself."

"This is a charade," I said. "None of us knows how to take care of ourselves."

Molly tossed me a look. "I oughta slap you," she said. She dragged me up the slanting A Deck to her suite, ripping open her closet, throwing gown upon gown on the bed.

"I can't," I said. "I've never worn women's clothes in my life and I certainly won't now."

"Don't be an ass."

"I can't."

"Join the charade," she said.

It was 1:48 AM by the clock on Molly's *escritoire*. She threw a red ballgown over me. "Why red?" I said.

"Because men always want to save a scarlet woman!" She plopped a heavy fur coat across my shoulders, turned up the collar, buttoned it at my throat, so recently occupied by Brice and Max, and plopped the broadest brimmed hat she could find on my head.

"This is cowardly, you know," I said.

"This," she corrected me, "is survival. You and your kind should understand that."

Me and my kind. How often had I heard that. But my kind had narrowed down to Edward, God knew where, locked down in the hold of the ship. "I don't care about my kind."

"I care about your kind," Molly said. She kissed me almost tenderly. "Come on, Queen Michael! Follow me! As far as I can tell, it's every man for himself, and hell will take the hindmost!"

Truly, I didn't want to die by drowning or freezing in the dark cold waters of the North Atlantic. I understood the code of old-style manners followed gamely by the rich gentlemen standing serenely on the decks, waving to their wives, lying in their teeth, assuring them they'd follow in the next lifeboats. In my red ballgown, I rode on Molly's arm with my moustache buried in her fur collar. I spied among the elegant men, searching for Edward.

On A Deck, Madeleine Astor's dog, Kitty, ran barking back and forth. From C Deck, the immigrant crowds in steerage raced up the stairs to first class, only to be trapped below stairs by the locked iron gates. *Titanic* was sinking fast into the water. The decks tilted sharply. The electric lights burned brightly. The band played. Flares hissed, flared, and burst overhead. Crystal goblets and flutes and bowls slid from the tables. The tables slid across the floors. Heavy machinery below was booming, breaking loose, sliding backwards toward the bow, pulling us down faster under its weight.

I noticed Molly carried an extra dress and coat and hat. "Do you intend to change?" I asked, overcome with the sarcasm of gallows humor. "Into something smart for a sinking?"

"It's for Edward."

"We must find him." My heart raced. My head spun. My humor changed. Everyone at that moment was leaving someone. Women, men, children. Separated. The seriousness of the situation made us all quiet for a moment, internal, listening to the cries of fate.

"We'll find him," Molly said.

Suddenly, the wild crowd pushed and shoved around us pressing us closer to portside Lifeboat 6 which was already descending over the side. In an instant, strong arms lifted me up into the air. It was Brice. "Come on, lady, here you go!"

"Brice," I said. "It's me."

"You!" He almost dropped me.

"Jump with me, Brice."

"It's my duty to stay."

"Fuck your duty. Save your life."

"I'm crew," he said solemnly. "You're a passenger."

"Don't be stupid."

He smiled ruefully. "Promise me one thing." He pulled me close to him.

"Anything."

Edward was not to be seen over Brice's shoulder.

"Live for me."

"Don't be British, Brice."

Disaster was upon us all.

"Live your life!"

Time slowed to a halt. Everything became deliberate, meaningful, absurd.

Brice smiled and said quite calmly, as if we were standing in a pub, "In New York. A new Turkish Bath. Run by the Police and Firemen Benevolent Association."

"Brice, we're sinking!"

"Go there!"

"Climb into this boat, and I won't have to make a donation in your memory."

"Rather!" He grinned like a sailor always expecting this inevitable moment.

"What's the place called?"

"The Everhard," he said.

Before I could say, "I must find Edward," Brice dropped me five feet over the side into the descending lifeboat. Molly, tossed over by Officer "Max" Maxwell, landed on top of me, all but crushing me, save for the drag she'd hauled along for Edward.

"Just shut up," she whispered.

Brice and Max stood together in the melee on the crowded deck. Over us all, a flare hissed up into the dark night and exploded.

Molly rose up and she shouted, making good use of her music hall voice, demanding another sailor. Just like Molly. Just like me. Demanding another sailor. "Throw me a sailor!" she bellowed. "I need a man to help row this boat full of sob-bin' women." She turned to me and whispered again. "You see? You'll be more help here rowing in a woman's dress than standing in your pants on deck singing hymns."

Brice tossed a sailor twelve feet down into our descending boat. It was Felix Jones. "I'm not a common sailor," Felix announced to everyone. "I'm a purser." I pulled my collar up and my hat brim down. "G'wan," Felix whispered. "I'd know you anywhere. We both can thank Mr. Brice and Officer Max and consider ourselves lucky."

As soon as we hit the water, Molly stood in the prow of the boat, like Washington crossing the Delaware, barking orders, commanding Felix and me and the 24 women in the boat to row for our lives. At that moment, the unsinkable Molly Brown became fixed in history and legend. I rowed with all my might, tears streaming down my face for my Edward, surely lost below decks.

It was a night so clear we could see stars reflecting themselves on a sea smooth as a mirror. The noise of the ship was enormous. People wailing, jumping, screaming in the night. Flare guns. Pistol shots. Random music, *nearer*, singing, *my God*, praying, *to thee*. Then like thunder, *Titanic* split in two. The bow sank almost instantly. There was a moment of almost absolute silence. It was 2:15 AM. Then thunder again. *Titanic*'s stern reared high in the water, bright, brilliant with light, phallic, magnificent in disaster, tall as a skyscraper. In a crashing avalanche, everything movable on the ship slid violently into the water. The postal clerks, dedicated to faithful delivery of their mail, were swept downwards in a tidal wave of envelopes and parcels. Hundreds and hundreds of people, a thousand, shouting, more than a thousand, screaming, were thrown into the cold sea thrashing in the 28 degree water. At 2:18 the lights in *Titanic*'s stern flickered and failed. *Titanic* stood vertically for ninety seconds, and at 2:20, the stern of the great ship slipped gurgling beneath the surface of the sea, sending up one immense white burst of steam toward the unblinking stars.

Two thousand people watched *Titanic* sink; 706 were in lifeboats.

Less than a mile away, an iceberg floated slowly on the current, a scrap of red and black paint smeared like whore's lipstick along its face.

Madame Ouspenskaya, too old to row, sat regally in the bow of Lifeboat 6, fully opposite Molly. Her face was impassive. Voices, passengers floating, swimming, freezing, sinking in the sea, cried out for help in the night.

I strained to hear, really not to hear, Edward's voice.

"Don't listen," Felix said. "They'd only swamp us."

Against their distant fading cries, our lifeboat lapped quietly on the ink-cold sea.

Molly wrapped the clothes meant for Edward around Mr. Astor's five-months-pregnant wife.

We rowed in the starry dark in silence. Other lifeboats floated on the quiet waters.

"Edward will be in one of the other boats," Molly said.

At 4:10, less than two hours after *Titanic*'s sinking, *Carpathia* loaded the first of the survivors up from the sea. Dawn and *Titanic* both lay eastwards behind us. *Carpathia*'s passengers, standing at first in awed silence, lined the rails as we were hoisted aboard in slings and bosuns' chairs. They cried for us. They pointed their fingers, and held their hands to their mouths, and lamented the boats, carrying only 5 or 25, designed for 40.

"You see," Maggie said, stripping her ballgown from me in the privacy of a stateroom. "You took no one's place."

Second Officer Charles H. Lightoller was the last survivor hoisted from the sea by creaking pulley to the deck of *Carpathia*. In all, only 706 souls of *Titanic*'s 2,228 passengers and crew survived the sinking.

1,522 died.

Including Edward Wedding.

My love. My lover.

Asleep in the deep, hopefully held in the strong arms of the Stoker.

The world was stunned. The only land station, immediately after the sinking of *Titanic*, powerful enough to receive the *Carpathia*'s messages sat atop Wanamaker's Department Store in Manhattan, where its 21-year-old operator, David Sarnoff, who was soon to found CBS, scribbled the garbled names of the survivors for release to the press.

On *Carpathia*'s return to New York, more than 10,000 people gathered on the Battery, at Manhattan's southern tip, as we passed, docking at 8:30 PM, at pier 54, at the foot of West 14th Street, where photographers' magnesium flares exploded like rockets in the dark of the spring night, and the silent movie cameras rolled.

Two days later, John Jacob Astor, millionaire, body number 124, was found in the sea, wearing men's clothes: a blue serge suit, a handkerchief monogrammed *JJA*, a brown flannel shirt, and brown boots with red rubber soles.

CPSIA information can be obtained at www.ICGtesting.com
Printed in the USA
LVOW041813280812

296367LV00001B/244/P

Chapter 14

32. Janet M Lernar, *Restoring Families*, Facilitators Guide, Living Free, Chattanooga, TN, 2000, 6.

Chapter 15

33. Franklin Graham, *Rebel With a Cause*, Thomas Nelson, Inc., 1995, 170.